THE TORTOISE AND THE TREE

ADAPTED FROM A BANTU FOLKTALE

JANINA DOMANSKA

GREENWILLOW BOOKS

A DIVISION OF WILLIAM MORROW & COMPANY, INC./NEW YORK

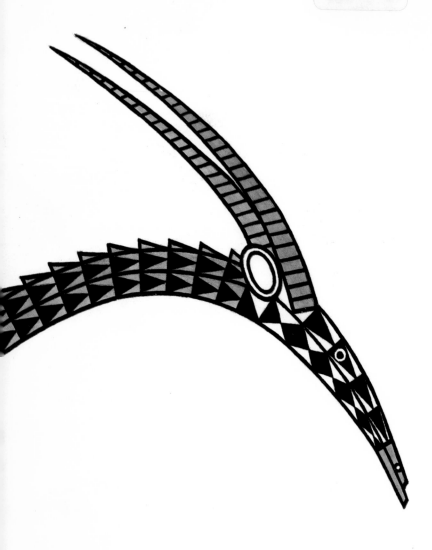

Library of Congress Cataloging in Publication Data
Domanska, Janina.   The tortoise and the tree.   Summary: A retelling of a Bantu folktale that explains how the tortoise got his patchwork shell.   [1. Folklore, Bantu] I. Title.
PZ8.1.D717To   [398.2] [E]   77-14572   ISBN 0-688-80132-3   ISBN 0-688-84132-5 lib. bdg.

FOR ANDREW

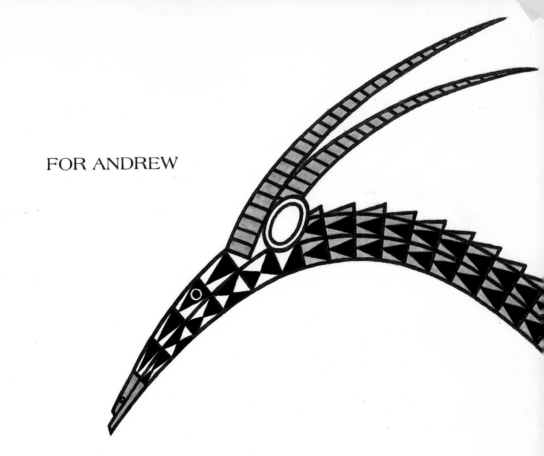

In a time of famine, all the animals gathered near a tree they knew would bear wonderful fruit when harvest time came.

 They built huts around the tree and waited for the fruit to ripen. When the fruit was ripe, they sent the hare to a nearby hill to ask Mavera, the High God, the name of the tree.

For the tree had a magic name and the fruit could
not be picked or eaten unless the name was spoken.

Mavera told the hare that the magic name
was "Uwungelema."

Then he said: "Go back, stand still before the tree, and say the name, and its fruit will be yours. But on your way home, you must not look back or you will forget the name."

The hare started for home and soon he heard the crackling of a branch. He could not help himself and looked back, and when he tried to remember the name of the tree, he could not.

"Uwungel—Uwuntul—Uwu—," he said to himself,

but the true name was gone from his mind.

The animals waited anxiously for the hare.
But when they asked for the name, he could only
stammer, "Uwu—Uwu—Uwu—," and they could
not have the fruit from the tree.

 The next morning, two buffaloes were sent to Mavera to try their luck. They learned the name and started for home.

As they trotted along, they heard the falling
of stones behind them and they looked back.

 And when they arrived at the tree, they too could
only mutter, "Uwu—Uwu—Uwu—," and of course,
the fruit remained forbidden.

 Then two gazelles were sent,

with the same result.

The next to go was the elephant.

He took great care to repeat the name

over and over again.

He was almost home when he heard a bird call.
He looked back to see where the sound came from
and forgot the name.

The last to go was the tortoise. Mavera told him
the name, but he also gave him a little bell, and said,
"I will put this around your neck. If you are tempted
to look back, the bell will ring and stop you."

The tortoise did, in fact, hear the rustling of a
snake and was frightened, but just as he was
about to turn his head, the bell rang to remind
him not to look back.

 When he reached home, he stood still beneath the tree, as Mavera had told him to, and spoke the magic name, Uwungelema.

The animals rushed to the tree. They picked
and ate the wonderful fruit.

 The hungry tortoise, however, could not reach the fruit and the greedy animals would not help him. Instead, they trampled on him, smashing his shell to pieces, and the tortoise died.

 The little ants who had witnessed the scene carried his body away and sang, "Knead the sand and mold the clay till he whom God made returns again."

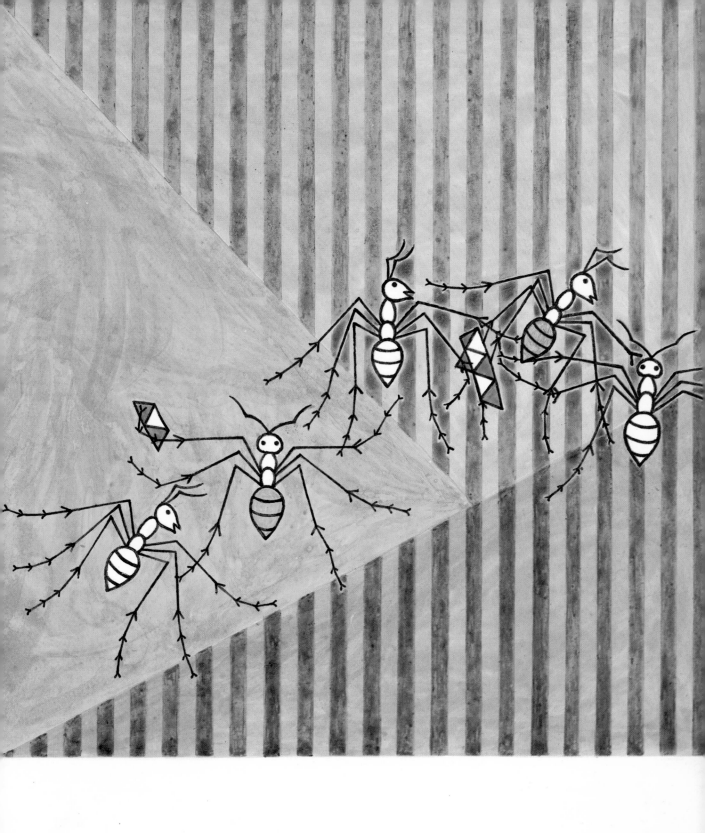

 As they sang, they put the tortoise's broken shell together, and he came back to life.

As soon as the tortoise regained his strength,

he uprooted the tree.

 When it fell, the animals, who were still feasting, were crushed beneath it. As for the tortoise, he has a patchwork shell to this very day.